LET GLASGOW FLOURISH

Maisie goes to Glasgow

Early morning Spring sunshine filled the street. Maisie Mackenzie felt its warmth through the glass as she sat at the window of her Granny's flat and watched for the postcat. It was Friday, and every Friday — without fail — the postcat brought her a letter from her Daddy. He was a famous explorer and, even as Maisie sat and waited, he was far away in the depths of a distant jungle.

"Discovering things," thought Maisie to herself.

The postcat turned the corner, looked up and saw Maisie. He gave her a wave, holding *two* letters in his paw. As he disappeared into the close entrance far below, Maisie jumped quickly from her chair and skipped to the door. She had it open long before the panting postcat reached the landing.

"Here you are, Maisie," he said with a chuckle. "One for you, and one for your Granny."

Maisie thanked him and ran into the kitchen, where Granny was making the breakfast porridge. Maisie examined the stamp on her letter. It was beautiful — a picture of a strange flower and a bright butterfly. She opened the envelope and started to read.

"Dear Maisie," wrote Daddy, "I have come a long way and am staying in a place that is rarely visited. Yesterday I met some huge lions in a clearing, and saw a chimp who can throw and catch coconuts. The food here is strange and peppery, not at all like your Granny's cooking! I hope you are . . . . ."

She was so busy reading, she hadn't noticed Granny putting her glasses on her nose and beaming at her own letter.

"My word, Maisie," said Granny, "this is from your Aunty Iza. Poor soul, how she manages to keep so cheery when she lives in Glasgow, I'll never know. Oh, she's been to the Sales, she says, and got a new hat, and her kitten Jimmy — he's your big cousin — is doing well at the University. Only Glasgow University, of course, but still. And your Uncle Willie has set up in business for himself, buying and selling. Buying and selling what, I wonder? She doesn't say. It's a while since I've seen them. I must let them know you're here."

As Granny read on, smiling to herself, sometimes nodding, sometimes shaking her head and saying, "Oh my! Fancy that!" Maisie put her letter carefully back in its envelope.

"Where's Glasgow, Granny?" she asked. "Is it in Edinburgh? Can I go there on the 23 bus?"

"Och no, pet. Glasgow is a big city, like Edinburgh." Granny laughed. "Well, not like Edinburgh. It's on the West Coast and you have to go by train to get there. Though why anyone would want to is quite beyond me."

"Are there interesting things to see there?" asked Maisie, becoming increasingly curious.

"I'm sure there must be. One or two anyway," replied Granny absently. "It's a great big place, much bigger than Edinburgh."

Maisie was intrigued. Bigger than Edinburgh!

Later that day, they went to Mrs McKitty's for dinner, which meant Maisie having her face scrubbed and her fur brushed, but the dinner was delicious and Maisie quickly cleaned her plate. For once, she didn't talk with her mouth full — to Mrs McKitty's approval. But she was thinking. Now she spoke.

"I think I'll go to Glasgow tomorrow, and explore there."

There was a moment's total silence.

Then Granny nearly choked on her mince and tatties. Mrs McKitty gasped.

"Glasgow!" spluttered Granny. "Glasgow! Och, Maisie, you *don't* want to go there!"

"Glasgow!" shrieked Mrs McKitty. "It's a dreadful place, not fit for an Edinburgh body at all. I never heard of such a thing. It's high time, young lady, that your Granny put your gas at a peep!"

With all the noise and commotion, Billy (Mrs McKitty's budgie) took fright and fluttered frantically round his cage, squawking, "Glasgow! Glasgow! Eek, Eek!" Once they had calmed down, Granny and Mrs McKitty explained to Maisie just how *awful* Glasgow was.

"Not a patch on Edinburgh . . . It's *Industrial* (Mrs McKitty shuddered as she said that) and it rains every day . . . Nothing good ever came out of Glasgow but the road to Edinburgh."

But Maisie was quite determined and, as it turned out that neither Granny nor Mrs McKitty had ever been there, insisted that she wanted to see for herself. Back in

their own flat, she won Granny round — pointing out that her own Daddy was an explorer, her Grandpa had been a seafarer, and that Granny was always telling her that there were Viking ancestors in the family. Against her better judgement, Granny agreed. She 'phoned Aunty Iza and arranged everything. Cousin Jimmy would meet Maisie at the Glasgow Station and she would stay with her Aunty and Uncle till Monday morning, when she would catch the train home. Granny packed Maisie's little wicker suitcase for her, with several changes of everything, "Just in case!" In the top, she popped a box of Edinburgh Rock for Aunty Iza.

Next morning, both Granny and Mrs McKitty (who was still muttering that "No Good" would come of this escapade) took Maisie to the Station. It was very busy, and they had to wait in a long queue before they could even buy the ticket. Granny slipped the ticket into Maisie's shoulder purse, tucked a clean hanky up her sleeve and made sure that Maisie had a note of Aunty Iza's address. Maisie was beginning to think that the adventure would *never* start, when — suddenly — the train was in, the passengers began to move, and she found herself in a carriage, with Granny and Mrs McKitty standing on the platform and reminding her to be *very* careful, to mind the traffic, her purse, her ticket, her manners, to ask a Policecat if she got lost. A shrill whistle blew and with a jolt and a shudder, the train began to move. Maisie waved to Granny and Mrs McKitty until they disappeared from view, then settled herself to enjoy the journey.

The carriage was full of football fans, very jolly and excited, dressed in striped hats and scarves. Maisie passed round Pan Drops Granny had given her for the train,

and listened with great interest to the talk about their teams. There were *two* big games in Glasgow that day, they told her, so the city would be crowded. Maisie began to feel quite excited, and even joined in the songs. She sang for both teams, but secretly believed that the one Archie supported — the Jam Tarts he called it — must be best!

At last the train reached Glasgow, and what a rushing and crushing began! Everyone spilled onto the platform and the great swaying, roaring football crowd, with poor wee Maisie jammed in its midst, surged towards the barrier and on out into the street. There, Maisie managed to break free. She found a quiet doorway and caught her breath, checked that she still had her case, her purse, her ticket! She ran back into the Station and handed it to the Ticket Collector, who remarked that she was "a credit to Edinburgh."

But there was no sign of Jimmy anywhere. Maisie walked about the Station for a few minutes, and decided that she would have to find her way to Aunty Iza's alone. Outside, she found herself in a fine big Square, bright with colourful flowers and with the sun shining just as warmly as it had been in Edinburgh. She skipped round the passers-by, chased a couple of pigeons, admired the statues of famous soldiers, poets and inventors, when suddenly! Her heart raced, she stopped skipping, she stared up. Right into the eyes of a *huge* white Lion. He seemed to be staring right back at Maisie. She thought of her Daddy, her brave Daddy, and wondered what he would do. Cautiously, she reached out her tiny paw and touched the Lion's great stone paw. Only a statue! Maisie laughed at herself, and skipped on her way.

She made her way down narrow streets and found herself outside a huge department store. Now, one thing Maisie really enjoyed was shopping. She had gone to Princes Street several times with Granny, though they never came back with much, because Granny was usually content to look and try. And Maisie loved to look and try, so she promptly marched into what Aunty Iza later told her was "the Largest Store in Scotland."

It was great fun riding up and down on the moving stairs; trying on the latest creations in the Hat department (and admiring herself in the mirror); testing settees and sofas for snoozability, and even a water-bed which wibbled and wobbled and made Maisie feel a bit woozy. At the Perfume Counter, she bought a bar of Lavendar soap for Mrs McKitty — to prove that nice things could come from Glasgow! The shop assistant gave Maisie a carrier bag to carry her things in and this gave her a jaunty air as she set out from the store in search of a tea-room.

"Exploring is thirsty work," she thought to herself.

The tea-room was a delight. It was very prettily decorated and very tranquil after the bustle of shopping. Maisie sat on a tall black chair and was served by a chatty waitress, who brought her tea and a cake stand with a choice of scones and iced fancies.

"So you've come all the way from *Morningside,* in Edinburgh," remarked the waitress. "My word! When I was a young pussy-cat, *I* used to go to Edinburgh, for the dancing at the Morningside Plaza. Imagine that! And what are you doing in Glasgow? Spending all your pocket money?"

"I've come to visit my Aunty Iza, but I don't know how to get there," admitted Maisie.

"Let me see," said the waitress, taking Maisie's note and reading the address. "Your Aunty lives in Hillhead — you should take the Subway, the Clockwork Orange."

Maisie looked puzzled, so the waitress explained.

"It's a funny wee train that runs under the ground," she laughed. "Right under the streets and shops, and tea-rooms."

Maisie jumped, and looked under her chair. But there was nothing there.

"Look for a sign like a big U," the waitress told her.

Maisie was most impressed. There was nothing like that in Edinburgh.

Outside the tea-room, she met a friendly Policecat, and he took her paw and led her across the road and all the way to St Enoch's Station. By the time they arrived,

The Clockwork Orange

she had told him all about the glen where she used to live, about her Daddy, her Granny, and even Mrs McKitty. The Policecat showed Maisie where to get her ticket and explained which way she was to go at Hillhead.

"We Highlanders have to look out for each other," he said, giving Maisie a wink. She didn't like to ask what he meant. She was *wee,* yes, but the Policecat was very tall.

Below ground, she didn't have to wait for long. When the train came in, Maisie understood why the waitress had called it a "Clockwork Orange." It was brightly painted and tiny. A kitten-sized train that rattled and swayed through a tunnel. The journey was thrilling and when Maisie discovered that the line ran in a circle, she was tempted to stay on until the train came right round again — but it was getting late and she didn't want Aunty Iza to worry about her.

It didn't take Maisie long to find Aunty Iza's street, and when she reached the right close, Number 20, her eyes grew large as saucers. It had beautiful floral tiles on the walls, which put Morningside to shame.

"Maybe they're very rich," wondered Maisie. "Perhaps they'll be angry with me for getting lost and being so late. Oh dear."

But when the door flew open, and Aunty Iza stood there, beaming at Maisie, she wasn't at all angry.

"Maisie Mackenzie," she cried, giving Maisie a hug and a kiss. "How you've grown. The last time I saw you, you were in a wee pram. I'm so pleased to see you. We were just going to 'phone your Granny to tell her you were lost. Jimmy's bus

got stuck in the football crowds and he missed you at the Station. But I can see you're a clever wee kitten to find your way here all by yourself. You're going to be an explorer like your Daddy, right enough. Come away in and meet your Uncle Willie and your Cousin Jimmy, while I put the kettle on."

At the fire side, Maisie explained what had happeneed, and the others laughed at her tale. Then Aunty Iza 'phoned Granny to let her know that Maisie had arrived

safely, and Jimmy promised that tomorrow he would give her a *guided* tour of Glasgow. That evening, after a fine Glasgow tea — which started with big bowls of broth and finished with lots of rich, fruity dumpling — Maisie sat on Uncle Willie's knee as he taught her some Glasgow songs. She thought one was especially funny. It went:

"Oh ye canny shove yer Granny aff a bus!
No, ye canny shove yer Granny aff a bus!
Oh ye canny shove yer Granny,
For she's yer Mammy's Mammy,
Ye canny shove yer Granny aff a bus!"

Maisie wondered if her own Granny had ever heard that song.

Jimmy played his mouth organ, and a penny whistle; Maisie danced a Highland Fling; and Aunty Iza sang some old Scots songs which brought a tear to everyone's eye. When Maisie passed round the Edinburgh Rock, Uncle Willie said that Maisie and the Rock were the two best things ever to come out of Edinburgh. It was a great night.

Next morning, straight after breakfast, Maisie set off with Jimmy to explore Glasgow. She thought it was wonderful to have a big cousin to look after her, and she held his paw tight.

They took the wee orange train into town, and Jimmy led Maisie to a place called *The Barras*. It was a big open-air market, with lots and lots of stalls, each piled high with everything imaginable.

"The Barras is famous all over the world, Maisie," said Jimmy. "You can buy almost anything here, new or second-hand."

Because of the crowd, Jimmy put Maisie up on his shoulders, from where she could see properly. They wandered from stall to stall and joined a big crowd at one, where a cat called Honest Fred was selling china. He threw a pile of plates up high in the air and caught them. Not *one* broke. Maisie was amazed. She was so impressed, she bought a present for Granny from Honest Fred. It was a cocoa mug, and on it was written, "The Best Granny in the World."

"As it's you, hen," said Honest Fred, tossing the mug high and deftly catching it in a paper bag, before giving it to Maisie, "Half-price. It's a bargain!"
Maisie put her bargain carefully in her carrier bag. At another stall she bought a postcard with a picture of Glasgow on it.

"That's for Daddy," she told Jimmy, as she popped it in the bag.
They wandered down to Glasgow Green and walked by the great River Clyde, and Jimmy told Maisie about the ships which, for generations, had sailed from here to trade with distant lands. Maisie wondered if her Grandpa had stood on this very spot. They took a bus to the Transport Museum, where Maisie sat on the upper deck of an open-topped tram and asked Jimmy for a return ticket to Auchenshuggle. When he said they should visit the Burrell Collection, she asked if it was anything like her collection of foreign stamps, or Archie's train numbers. Jimmy laughed. It was like nothing she had ever imagined.

"There's more here than at The Barras," whispered Maisie, gazing round at a vast array of priceless paintings, sculptures and other treasures.
They had a picnic outside and Maisie chatted to the Highland Cattle, who gazed

through their matted fringes at her and told her that they missed the mountains of the north, the heather, the cry of the golden eagle and the musical lilt of their native Gaelic tongue. Maisie agreed with them, as she munched a mutton pie.

"Granny will be surprised," laughed Maisie.

That evening, Jimmy took Maisie to an Indian Restaurant. It was called the Catmandu, was very exotic, and they were attended by a majestic cat with a jewelled turban on his head.

"Nothing too hot for you, little kitten," he purred. "This is your first real curry and you are very small."

Maisie revelled in the surroundings, the attention and, of course, the meal. It was a real adventure. Fluffy white rice, little cubes of lamb in a spicy sauce, bowls of sweet pickle and chutney, and crispy pancakes called Poppadums. She decided to teach Granny to make curry.

By the end of the meal, she was so full that Jimmy had to put her up on his shoulders again, and carry her home.

Next morning, after breakfast, Aunty Iza said that Uncle Willie would give her a lift to the Station, so, with Jimmy bringing Maisie's things, they went downstairs to the street. What a surprise — not a car, not even a taxi . . . . Uncle Willie was sitting up on a cart, piled high with all sorts of junk and scrap, and he was holding the reins of a horse! Uncle Willie was a *Rag and Bone Man!*

Maisie climbed up beside him, Jimmy put her case and carrier bag on the back, Aunty Iza kissed Maisie and made her promise to come back soon. Maisie waved

and waved as the cart jolted and rumbled through the streets. She laughed to herself. *Whatever* would Mrs McKitty say if she could see Maisie now?

At the Station, she wrote her postcard to Daddy — "Have explored Glasgow, met a Lion, saw a barker throw and catch a cocoa mug, ate a curry. Love and kisses from Maisie." She posted it and Uncle Willie saw her safely onto the train. As it sped back to Edinburgh, Maisie curled up happily and closed her eyes.

"Glasgow is a *big* place," was her last thought as she fell asleep.

Back home, she told Granny and Mrs McKitty everything. They were pleased with their presents, but when Mrs McKitty heard about the tiled close, she said nothing. Later, as Maisie sat on Granny's knee, Granny told her how much she'd missed her.

"I've got so used to you running around the place, pet," said Granny.

"It was great fun, Granny," purred Maisie, sipping her cocoa. "But Aunty Iza taught me an old saying, which she said all travellers should remember: 'East, West, Home's Best'."

"That's true," agreed Granny.